RANGE WAR IN C MINOR

A Clay Jared Western

R. Annan

Range War in C Minor
Copyright 2015 by R. Annan
WGA Reg. #: R31634 (11/3/15)

Edition 1.1
One Vision Publishing
ISBN: 978-1-942338-44-4 (e-Book)
ISBN: 978-1-942338-43-7 (Print)

Western books by R. Annan:

Fight for The Lazy M
The Gunfighter in Winter
Long Ride to Hell's Kitchen
Owl Hawks
Gunfight at Barfield Springs
Shootout at Sanctuary City
Last Days of a Gunfighter
Red Bandana
Copperhead Moon
Cowboys of the Box R
Prisoners of Brimstone Pass

To

JAG, Jim W., Regrae, John T., Soine, Bill, Mike McMullen
and Nancy Taylor

Thank you for your kind words of support.

It's a pleasure to ride with you.

1.

It was Friday evening and pianist Claire Adams was standing backstage at the Coates Opera House in downtown Kansas City with her companion Celia Grant. The two were a contrast in color. Claire was a tall, dark-haired, brown-eyed beauty, while Celia was a petite, blue-eyed blonde. And where Claire was relaxed and self-controlled, Celia was volatile and excitable.

"Just look at that crowd, Claire. It's much bigger than last night," Celia giggled.

It was going to be the young pianist's final performance in Kansas City before returning to New York.

"And that nice looking man is there again, Claire. He's been front row, center seat, every night."

Claire looked past the proscenium to the front row. It was true. That same man was there. He had appeared at the Monday night opening and returned each evening after that.

"He must really like Chopin," Celia remarked.

"Yes," Claire agreed, "he really must."

The playbill promised an all-Chopin recital with select waltzes, preludes, nocturnes, ballads and etudes.

"Perhaps he's interested in you as well," Celia giggled.

Claire stared at the man. He was perhaps ten years older than her and very nice looking. His brown hair was quite long for a man of the East, so Claire took him to be a westerner. His face was tanned by the sun. It was a nice face, not what you would call handsome, but nice.

Before Claire Adams could respond to Celia's remark, her agent, Gerald Remy, hurried up to her holding a piece of paper. He nodded quickly to Celia then turned to Claire with a look of concern on his face.

"Claire, darling, I'm afraid I'll have to leave you here to finish the concert on your own."

"Why? What's wrong, Gerald?"

"I was just handed this wire. Mother is terribly ill and is asking for me. I'm sorry, but I must go back to New York."

"Oh, I'm so sorry, too, Gerald. Yes, you must return as soon as possible."

"I'll take the next train east," Remy said. "But there's no reason for you and Celia to rush back. Relax a few days."

This was Claire's last performance after four straight days and she felt a little tired. A week or so spent relaxing and seeing the sights around Kansas City seemed like a good idea.

"Perhaps I will, Gerald," Claire said. "But do go. Catch that train. And good luck!"

Remy kissed both girls on the cheek and rushed off. He was a short, rotund, balding man and he waddled like a duck as he hurried away.

At about that time the curtain parted. Claire gave Celia a hug and walked slowly out onto the stage to thunderous applause. She faced the audience and nodded, then went to the grand piano center stage and sat down to play. Two hours later, she stood and faced the proscenium again. The applause was loud and long.

She gave out a big sigh. The concert was over. The tour had ended.

It had been a long slow trek starting out in New York, in the spring of 1886, and travelling to Pittsburgh, Cincinnati and St. Louis. They finally ended up at the Coates Opera House in Kansas City.

Back in her dressing room, Claire was met by two uniformed ushers carrying huge bouquets of flowers.

"You have an admirer," Celia said. She was giddy with excitement.

As Claire bent over to smell the flowers, she saw the attached envelope and opened it.

"What does it say?" Claire asked as she sat down.

"It says, 'Can I come in?'"

"Who is it from?"

"It doesn't say," Celia answered.

Just then, there was a knock on the dressing room door.

Celia rushed to open it.

"Oh!" Celia Grant was speechless.

She stood staring at the man who had sat each day in the front row. He wore a white Stetson and his suit pants were tucked into a fancy pair of cowboy boots.

"Can I come in?"

"Please," Celia said.

The man removed his hat and entered the dressing room. He looked handsomer close up. He wasn't tall but he had wide shoulders. Celia Grant seemed to be transfixed as she stared at the man with eyes wide and mouth open.

The man, however, was staring at Claire Adams.

"Miss Adams," the man said. "My name is Lee Compton. I am a most ardent admirer of yours, ma'am."

Claire stood up to face the man. "Thank you for the flowers, Mr. Compton. They're lovely."

"I must say, Miss Adams, your playing of the Chopin C Minor Etude was absolutely incredible. I came every day to hear you play it."

Claire smiled. "Yes. Celia and I noticed." Then she added, "And thank you for the compliment, sir."

"Lee. Please call me Lee," Compton said. "And you too, Miss Celia."

Compton's rich, western tone almost had Celia Grant in a swoon. She couldn't take her eyes off the man.

"Miss Adams," Compton said, "would you and Miss Celia do me the honor of dining with my mother and me at the Osmond Hotel? It's just around the corner."

"I would be honored, Mr. Compton."

"Wonderful. I'll be waiting out on the street, then." Compton bowed and left.

"Oh, my God!" Celia cried. She repeated it three times.

"Calm down now," Claire Adams said, laughing. "He isn't God, you know."

"He's such a gentleman," Celia said. "And so handsome, too. I could just die the way he looked at you."

"Oh, Celia. You're such a romantic."

In half an hour, they were sitting at a table in the Osmond Hotel with Lee Compton and his mother, a white-haired, elegant looking woman of about sixty.

The two girls from New York eventually learned that Ardis Compton was a widow of old western pioneer stock. Her husband had left her a 300,000-acre ranch with over 150,000 head of cattle. The ranch was called the Circle C and it was about fifty miles south of Ellsworth, Kansas. Someday it would all belong to her son, Lee.

Ardis Compton glared sternly across the table at Claire Adams and bluntly asked, "Have you ever ridden a horse, Miss Adams?"

"As a matter of fact, no, I haven't, Mrs. Compton."

"Have you ever shot a gun or a rifle?"

"I've never had that pleasure, ma'am," Claire responded, looking a bit embarrassed.

Ardis Compton gave her son a cold look as if to imply that this girl was not qualified to be a Compton. As for Lee, he couldn't take his eyes off Claire. To make things worse, much to the annoyance of his mother, the girl from New York boldly smiled right back at her son. It was as if Ardis Compton was not even in the room.

Mrs. Compton abruptly stood and harrumphed as loudly as she could. She tossed her napkin into her soup bowl.

"Lee, I have a headache. I'm going up to my room." Without another word, she turned and left.

"Your mother is very passionate," Claire said.

"I'm afraid my mother is a bit overprotective," the rancher replied. "I'm all she has."

"I understand," Claire replied.

Afterwards Compton took Claire and Celia for a tour of the town. They sat in a carriage and rode around looking at such sights as the railroad bridge across the Missouri, the

Majestic Restaurant, the Quality Hill Residential area, and the cattle yards.

Later Compton made it clear that he wanted to see Claire again. "Do you have to go back to New York right away?"

"No, I don't have to," Claire said.

Celia Grant cut in, "We have plenty of time, Mr. Compton. And Claire needs a rest."

"Then you two should come to stay at the Circle C for a while as my guests," Compton suggested.

"Will there be cowboys there?" Celia asked.

Compton laughed. "Oh, yes. Quite a few."

"I'm dying to meet a cowboy," the naive girl giggled.

"Then come visit the Circle C. Please do."

"Alright," Claire said, "we would love to visit your ranch."

They quickly mapped out the travel plans.

"Mother and I will be leaving tomorrow," the rancher explained. "You two will need to get some more suitable outfits for ranch life. Gable's Mercantile in downtown

Kansas City has everything you'll need. I'll notify them to put the cost on my account."

"Oh, no," Celia insisted. "No need for that, Lee. We'll handle that ourselves."

The rancher insisted strongly so Claire finally gave in to his wishes.

They planned the route of travel.

"You'll take the train as far as Ellsworth," Compton went on to explain. "I'll meet you with a buckboard at the train depot and bring you the rest of the way to the Circle C."

"Gosh," Celia cried in excitement. "A buckboard!"

"Calm down, Celia," Claire laughed.

Compton continued. "We'll lay overnight at Mrs. Simpson's Bed and Breakfast in Fogelsburg. I'll let her know we're coming. The next day we'll be at the Circle C."

"Alright," Claire said. "I'll settle up here, buy some things, and come behind you, then. Is that alright?"

"That's fine," Compton said, smiling. He was a very happy man.

He kissed the girls' hands, bowed and left.

The next day, a Saturday, Celia spoke to Claire about a book she had read concerning an Englishwoman in India.

"She wore things called jodhpurs, wore a man's shirt, boots, hat and a vest."

"Yes, I've seen pictures of that. It's called a riding habit," Claire replied. "Very good, Celia."

That Monday they boarded the train for Ellsworth wearing dresses instead of jodhpurs and boots. It was clear that that type of outfit was made for outdoor activities such as riding horses but not for sitting in a train car.

So they packed them away for future use.

2.

The train stopped at several places, but the most impressive one was Abilene, about seventy miles east of Ellsworth. While passengers got off and on, Claire and Celia sat in the passenger car waiting for the train to move on again.

Suddenly Celia let out a gasp.

"Look, Claire," the girl from New York said, pointing out the window towards the train platform, "real honest-to-goodness cowboys! Aren't they something to see?"

Claire laughed at her friend.

"Celia, you've been reading too many of those awful western romance pulp magazines."

"Come, now, Claire, you have to admit they look, well, so noble. Doesn't the way they dress and carry themselves and sit on a horse remind you of the knights of old?"

"Sorry, but no," Claire chuckled.

"Come, let's go out there and take a closer look at them. The train won't be leaving for a while."

"No, foolish girl! I will not go out there."

"Then I will!"

Celia Grant jumped up and quickly walked to the end of the car and out onto the platform of Abilene's train station.

She became aware of gunfire in the distance. An out of tune piano was playing in a saloon near the depot. Life beyond the depot was bustling like a beehive. People, unseen but close, laughed, shouted, growled and complained.

When the cowboys on the platform saw Celia Grant come rushing from the train, they immediately stopped their horsing around and stood still as stones, staring at her. After a moment of taking in her beauty, they tipped their wide brimmed hats in a graceful salute.

"Howdy, ma'am," a tall, lean, handsome one said. "Kin I be of any assistance to ya?" He removed his hat to reveal his long, wavy auburn hair. It hung down to his shoulders, giving him a wild look.

Celia Grant walked straight up to the cowboy. He backed off a few steps, caught completely off guard, staring at her as if she were something delicate he didn't want to step on. He gave her a wide smile.

"You're a cowboy, aren't you?"

The cowboy chuckled and smiled.

"Yes, ma'am," the young cowboy said. "I am a cowboy."

"You're gorgeous," the girl blurted out.

The cowboy didn't know what to say. He shifted his hat to his left hand, held it at his side, and stared down at her in wonder.

"My momma always said I was the ugliest of the lot," the cowboy replied.

"Well, she was wrong," Celia said seriously. "You are absolutely gorgeous. I could eat you up."

The other cowboys looked on with keen interest. They had never seen anything like this before.

"Ah, ma'am," the cowboy said. "Are you alright?"

Celia Grant reached up, pulled the cowboy's head down to her level, and planted a long, hot kiss on his lips. She then pulled a perfume-scented handkerchief out of her dress pocket and tucked it into his gunbelt then turned and ran back to the train.

For a moment, the cowboy was dazed and unable to move. Reaching down slowly to his gunbelt, he pulled the handkerchief out and held it to his face, inhaling its sweet fragrance. The other cowboys broke out into a chorus of cheers and came over and gathered around their comrade, patting him on the back in envy.

The train began to pull out of the Abilene depot with Celia Grant waving from the car window. The cowboy came running up to look in at her.

"I love you, ma'am! Will ya marry me?" he shouted.

"Yes!" Celia shouted back.

Everyone in the car looked and laughed.

The cowboy ran alongside the car until it pulled away, leaving him waving in the distance.

Claire Adams stared at her friend.

"You are a most naughty little girl, Celia Grant. I hope your mother and father never hear of this."

"You won't tell them, will you?"

"Of course not," Claire laughed.

3.

They arrived at Ellsworth early in the day and were met by a comely young cowboy. He was waiting alongside the platform with a buckboard that had a saddled horse tied to it.

"I'm Bob Marsh," the cowboy said. "Mr. Compton couldn't come."

"Oh? Is something wrong?"

"His mother wasn't feeling well, ma'am."

The porter brought the women's bags out and piled them on the platform. Marsh quickly loaded them onto the back of the buckboard.

Celia Grant watched him with interest.

"Do all cowboys wear a gun?" she asked him when he was finished loading the bags.

"Yes, ma'am."

"Why?"

Marsh chuckled. "Well, fer lots a reasons, ma'am."

"Like what, for instance?"

Bob Marsh smiled down at Celia Grant. Their eyes locked for a moment.

"Well, let's see." Marsh considered the question. He took his hat off and scratched his head, pretending to be deep in thought. "There's shootin' rattlesnakes, an' two-footed snakes, an' robbin' banks, an' things like that, fer instance."

He paused to see the effect his words had on the girl. She looked amazed.

"Really?"

"Oh, sure!" Marsh continued. "An' then there's shootin' coyotes and cheatin' girlfriends and their boyfriends. Stuff like thet."

Celia suddenly caught on and hit Marsh playfully on the arm.

"You're playing with me, Mr. Marsh."

"Ouch! Ma'am, you sure got a punch!" They all laughed.

Marsh pointed to the pile of traveling bags.

"Looks like you all will be stayin' a while."

"Two weeks at most, Mr. Marsh," Claire said.

Marsh looked at Celia Grant. "Sorry ta hear thet, ma'am." The girl caught his meaning and so did Claire. The cowboy couldn't keep his eyes off the perky little blonde.

Suddenly Claire said, "How rude of me, Mr. Marsh. My name is Claire Adams and this is my friend, Celia Grant."

Marsh chuckled. "I know, Miss Claire. Mr. Compton already told me."

Without warning Marsh grabbed Celia under the arms and swung her up on the seat of the buckboard.

"Oh, dear, Mr. Marsh," Celia purred. "You are very strong, aren't you?"

"Shucks, ma'am. Not really."

He helped Claire up, then went around to the other side and climbed up next to Celia. He took up the reins and gave them a snap. The one-horse buckboard moved down the road past the outskirts of Ellsworth. Soon the loud, raucous sounds of that wild cattle town faded in the distance.

In short time they were out in open country on an old coach road that led to Fogelsburg. It wound through stands of pine and aspen trees and across wide expanses of prairie grass.

Colors began to appear. The land took on a deep green hue. Wildflowers grew in abundance, adding touches of red, yellow, pink and blue. The sky was a huge, blue dome above, and the clouds, painted a pale pink by the sun, hung above purple colored mountains that rose in the distance. It literally took both city girls' breath away.

"This is so beautiful," Claire said.

"You won't think so in a few minutes," Bob Marsh chuckled.

"Why not?" Celia asked.

The cowboy pointed to a cluster of clouds with dark underbellies.

"It's a comin' our way, ladies!"

In a few moments, they got hit with a rainsquall. The wind picked up, forcing them to hold on to their bonnets. It quickly passed, leaving them a bit wet.

"What do you do at the ranch, Mr. Marsh?" Celia asked.

"I wrangle mostly."

"What's that?"

The young cowboy chuckled at her innocence.

"I fool around with the cows. Brand 'em. Break wild horses. Move herds. Stuff like thet."

"It sounds exciting," Celia said.

"Not so much. I seldom git ta see such pretty ladies as you an' Miss Claire, ma'am. Mostly there's nobody ta kiss but an old cow."

Celia Grant laughed.

"Say, Miss Celia," the cowboy said. "Kin you read book words?"

"Yes, I can, Mr. Marsh. Why do you ask?"

"Well, I got this book an' it has pictures in it of men with horny hats. They're all half-nekkid an' carry big, long knives," Bob Marsh said.

"Oh, you must mean Vikings," Celia said. She suddenly realized that the cowboy couldn't read.

"Do you know anything about them, ma'am?"

"Yes. They lived centuries ago and were very brave fighters," Celia said. "When they died in battle, they were placed on a raft with their swords on their chests and a dead pig at their feet. The raft was set on fire and pushed out to sea. That's how they buried their dead."

"Yeah, thet's what ol' Del Benton told me. He kin read a little. I can't. I showed him the book."

"Who is Mr. Benton?" Celia asked.

"He's the ramrod of the Circle C," Marsh replied.

Claire sat smiling and quietly listening as Celia and the young cowboy talked. Her friend had never seemed happier.

All of a sudden, the young cowboy laughed.

"What's so funny?" Celia asked him.

"Them there Vikin's. They sure knew how ta give a man a send-off, didn't they, ma'am?"

"Yes, they did at that, Mr. Marsh," the young girl replied.

She liked this cowboy. He was a breath of fresh air compared to those stuffy, boring city boys she had met.

And he wore a gun!

4.

By the time they reached Fogelsburg it was late in the afternoon and everyone was pretty well covered with dust. The women were sore from jouncing up and down on the hard buckboard seat.

They rode down the main street past a saloon called the Black Bull to the other edge of town where Marsh tied up in front of a whitewashed, two-story, clapboard house. A sign out front read "Widow Simpson's Bed and Breakfast".

Mrs. Simpson herself came out to greet them with a happy smile.

"Hello, ladies. I'm Widow Simpson. Please come in."

Inside, Mrs. Simpson showed them to a large room with twin brass beds and a stand-alone bathtub.

"This here is the bridal suite," the chubby, white-haired, middle-aged woman said, always smiling. "Mr. Compton has reserved it especially fer you girls ta stay as long as ya need ta."

"We'll be leaving in the morning," Claire said.

"Breakfast is at seven."

"Thank you," Claire said. "You are most kind."

Bob Marsh and the widow carried the luggage up, then tramped back downstairs.

"How have ya been, Bobby-boy?" the widow asked.

"Fine, Mrs. Simpson."

"You hungry, son?"

"I wouldn't mind a shot at yer apple-rhubarb tart, ma'am."

They went into the kitchen. The cowboy sat down at the table while Mary Simpson made a fresh pot of coffee.

There was a man out back chopping wood. She stepped out and told him to start pumping up water from the well for the bathtub. She put a large, galvanized basin on the stove to heat the water when it was brought in. Finally, she cut Marsh a piece of tart and sat across the table from him.

"Them two girls? Where they from, Bob?"

"Mr. Compton says New York."

Widow Simpson shook her head.

"This ain't no place fer them at a time like this, Bob."

"You mean with the Box M problem?"

"Thet's jest what I mean. I bet they ain't never seen a dead body in their whole life."

"I suppose yer right, ma'am."

"Well, the chances are they're gonna see plenty if this thing blows up."

Bob Marsh nodded.

"An' then there's his momma. Them girls ain't gonna feel so welcome when she gits done with 'em."

"Yer right there, ma'am. She's don't like no woman near him unless she brings one in herself. Thet's fer sure."

The widow sighed. "Well, it ain't my worry."

Marsh finished his coffee and tart and stood up.

"I'll sleep in the barn, ma'am," the cowboy said. "Thanks fer the grub."

Marsh drove the buckboard around to the back of the house and into the barn. He unhitched the buckboard horse, watered and fed it some oats, then locked it in a hay stall. He did the same for his own horse.

After that, he walked up to the Black Bull Saloon.

On the way he noticed two men watching him from the other side of the street, keeping pace with him as he walked along. He recognized them as Box M men.

If there were some Circle C men in the Black Bull, he would be all right. If not, then he was in big trouble and so were the women.

5.

Clay Jared rode across a field of sage and prairie grass, then up on a rise overlooking the town of Folgelsburg. From where he sat in the saddle, he had a good view of the entire area. He noticed a one-horse buckboard traveling in from the east at a slow pace. It had a driver and two women with an extra horse tied behind.

Because of their dresses, he thought the women were probably dance hall girls but when they stopped at a big, white house, he checked that thought. Maybe they were travelers. A portly woman came out to greet them as if they were important people. He watched with interest for a while as the woman and the driver, plainly a cowboy, carried the luggage in.

They had to be travelers and special ones at that.

Jared looked the town over. It wasn't any different from any other town he had come across. They all had a bar, a jail and a graveyard. Some of the bigger towns, like Dodge, even had an opera house.

"Come on, pal," Jared said to his horse. "Let's go get a beer."

He flicked the reins and rode slowly down into Fogelsburg. Ten minutes later he tied up in front of the Black Bull Saloon. He'd have a few drinks and go rent a stall at the local stable for him and his horse. He didn't like to sleep in hotels. They were usually noisy and full of drunks, and men shot each other over painted ladies. Often there was a cowboy snoring, sounding like a bull in rut, in the next room.

He walked into the Black Bull. The bar was on the right. There was a large crock of pickled cucumbers and a bowl of boiled eggs on it. Lined up next to that was a jar of jerky sticks. All the snacks were a quarter eagle. The smell of stale tobacco juice rose up from the spittoons under the bar.

The bartender, a paunchy, bald man with a beard and a soiled apron, came over.

"New, aincha?"

"Just passing through."

"They're hiring out at the Circle C an' the Box M, if yer interested in wranglin'. But if'n I was you, I'd stay away from both of 'em."

Jared nodded. He scratched the week old stubble on his chin. "Thanks for the information."

He stared at the crock for a few moments.

"Go ahead, mister, it ain't poisoned," the bartender laughed.

Jared laid a quarter eagle on the bar, grabbed the wooden tongs and picked out a cucumber. He bit it in half and chewed away.

"You'll want a drink after thet," the bartender chuckled.

"Yeah," Jared gasped. The cucumber was peppery hot.

"What'll ya have, rotgut?"

"Naw. A local brew," Jared said.

The bartender turned to look at an array of different shaped bottles on a sideboard behind him. He began going down the list in a boring monotone.

"Well, we got Rub-of-the-Brush, a potato beer, and Witch's Tit, a hard cider, an' another beer called Sodom and Gomorrah. Pig's Patootie is made of I don't know what. And we also got Mom's Medicine. I wouldn't touch Mom's Medicine unless ya wanna crap yer pants."

"Rub-of-the-Brush," Jared said. It was like playing Russian roulette.

"Good pick." The bartender chuckled.

He handed Jared an amber colored flip-top.

Jared popped it open. It spewed foam. He waited a second and took a sip.

"Not too bad," he said. "My compliments to the brewer."

Someone stood next to him at the bar. Jared gave the man a glance and saw it was the cowboy he'd seen driving the buckboard.

More out of curiosity than politeness, Jared said, "Hi!" The cowboy returned the greeting with a smile and a nod.

"What'll ya have, Bob?" the bartender asked.

"Gimme a whiskey, Ted."

The bartender grabbed a bottle of rotgut and poured Bob Marsh a shot. The cowboy placed an eagle on the bar.

Suddenly two men appeared. The thin one pushed Jared aside as he elbowed his way between him and the young cowboy's right side. The second man, big and heavy, stood crowding the kid on the left.

Jared saw what had happened and he knew what was about to happen. He dropped his right hand down by his Colt.

"Well, well," the big one on the kid's left sneered. "If'n it ain't little Bobby Marsh of the Circle C. How's it goin', kid?" He gave out a sarcastic laugh.

"What the hell you want, Slade?" Marsh growled.

"Who's the pretty thangs ya dropped off at the Simpson place, Marsh?" the thin, lean one asked.

"None a yer business, Turell."

"I'm makin' it my business," Turell insisted. "Maybe I'll jest mosey down there an' ask 'em fer a dance." He laughed at his own brand of humor.

"You better not try thet!" Marsh said coldly.

"What's their names, Bob?" the big one asked.

"Like the kid said, it's none of your business, fat ass!" Jared said, turning to face Slade and Turell.

For a moment, the two were caught off guard. Slade saw Jared smiling and didn't like it.

"Who the hell are you, mister?"

"I'm with Bob," Jared said, "and I'm the guy who's gonna kick yer ass if you don't move on."

Marsh looked at Jared. "Do I know ya, mister?"

"Sure, you do, kid. I'm your pard."

Marsh caught on and shrugged. "Oh, right." He turned to Slade, "He's my pard, asshole. So take yer Box M asses outta my face."

"Why you little runt! I'm a-goin' ta drill yer little ass here and now!" Slade dropped his hand down by his holster.

"No, ya ain't," Ted the bartender said. "I got my hand on a scattergun. You pull iron in here, Slade, an' I'll blow ya all over thet wall back there."

"Sure, Ted, sure," Slade said, backing away. He sneered at Bob Marsh. "C'mon outside an' say thet, kid. You an' yer big mouth pard. Jest the four of us. Or are ya afraid?"

"I ain't afraid a no Box M man!" Marsh growled. "Hell, let's go."

The young cowboy walked quickly out through the batwing doors onto the porch. Slade and Turell were close on his heels.

Ted looked at Jared and scowled.

"Hell, ya don't even know the kid."

Jared took another swig of Rub-of-the-Brush.

"I'll finish the rest in a few minutes, Ted," Jared said and walked outside.

A mixture of a dozen or more people, some cowboys, some painted ladies and some citizens, were already in watching position on the porch. Jared squeezed past them and stepped out into the road next to Bob Marsh.

"I'm Clay Jared, kid."

"I'm Bob Marsh. I ride fer the Circle C."

They shook hands. Jared stared up the road at Slade and Turell, about thirty feet away.

"Which one is the fastest, kid?"

"Turell, the tall bean pole facing you."

"Then he's mine," Jared said. "If you don't mind."

"You sure? He's greased lightnin', mister."

"Yeah, I'm sure." Jared eyeballed Turell for a moment then yelled, "Hey, Turell, didn't you get arrested for molesting sheep up in Belcher Springs last year?"

Turell's face turned purple with rage. The worst insult a cattleman could have tossed at him was to be called a sheep lover.

"Draw, you son of a bitch!"

Turell was fast. His hand was a blur as he drew. The roar of guns cut the evening air and echoed down Fogelsburg's main street, into the alleyways and out onto the prairie grass fields beyond.

Jared beat Turell by a second and shot him in the chest. The bullet slammed into his lean frame like a sledgehammer and sent him skidding on his back ten feet along the road. He strained to get up but fell back and died.

Slade's shot took Bob Marsh in the side and spun him sideways. The young cowboy fanned off a snap shot that hit the big man in his right arm. Slade dropped his gun and reached for his second gun with his left hand. The kid saw it coming. He was on his knees when he fanned off a second shot. It hit Slade square between the eyes.

For a moment, Slade stood looking dazed. Then his eyes slowly looked up at the sky and his knees buckled like a door shutting in the wind. He hit the road hard and fell forward on his face in a heap.

For a moment, everyone was quiet, then someone yelled, "The kid! He's hurt!"

Bob Marsh sat in the road looking white as a sheet. Jared holstered his Colt, walked up to him and knelt down. The young cowboy was holding his left side as he tried to put his gun away.

"Shucks," the young cowboy muttered. "Thet bastard Slade tagged me good." He inhaled deep and exhaled slowly. "Get me down ta Mrs. Simpson's, will ya, Jared?"

"Sure thing, kid."

As Jared helped Bob Marsh to his feet, someone yelled from the crowd.

"You better run, mister! Snake Norton will be coming ta get ya!"

6.

Jared got his horse, helped the young cowboy up into the saddle and then swung up behind the cantle to keep him from falling. Marsh grabbed the saddle horn and hung on as they made their way slowly down the road to Mrs. Simpson's house. When they got there, Jared dismounted and lowered Marsh to the ground.

The women came running out.

When Celia saw the blood on the cowboy's left side she cried out, "Oh, God! Is he hurt bad?"

"I'm a-dyin' fer sure, Miss Grant," the young cowboy muttered in a painful voice. "Kin I git a kiss before I go?"

"Yes, Bob," the young girl replied. She kissed the cowboy on the cheek.

"Is thet all I get?" Marsh asked just before he collapsed in Jared's arms.

"Git the poor critter inside before he bleeds ta death," the widow said. She turned and ran into the house as fast as her old legs would carry her.

Jared picked Marsh up and carried him behind her. He followed her into the kitchen and set the wounded cowboy in a chair. The old lady got the medicine box.

"Git his shirt open!" she said calmly.

Jared opened the boy's shirt to expose the wound. Celia knelt beside him and held his hand, staring at the ugly wound.

"Oh, God! He's going to die!"

"No, he ain't," Widow Simpson said as she opened the medicine box. "This ain't the first cowboy I had ta patch up, an' I ain't ever lost one yet. An' I ain't gonna lose you, Bobby Marsh!"

The old lady sloshed some antiseptic solution on a rag, intending to swab the wound front and back where it had passed clean through the flesh.

"This is gonna burn like the blazes, Bob," she said. "So ya better holler loud."

And he did. Bob Marsh howled like a wounded banshee.

"Damn, thet sure felt good," he said, gasping for air.

"You sure kin sing pretty, Bobby-boy," Mrs. Simpson chuckled.

"Is he hurt bad?" Claire asked.

"It's bad enough," the widow said. "The good news is thet it went clean through, in and out. He's lost a lot a blood, but it's stopped bleedin' now, which is also a good thing."

Bob Marsh looked up. "I'm fine," he said.

"We'll see about thet," Mrs. Simpson said.

"Jest toss me in the back of tha buckboard an' my pard here kin drive us on ta tha Circle C. Heck, it ain't but thirty miles away."

"You ain't goin' no place taday, young man," Mrs. Simpson said. "Maybe tomorrow. Yer young an' strong so you'll heal quick, I reckon." She turned to Jared. "Kin you git him upstairs?"

"Sure."

"Then follow me."

Jared got Marsh standing and helped him along. They followed Mrs. Simpson upstairs to a small bedroom and laid him down on the bed. Celia Grant sat beside him holding his hand. The widow, Jared and Claire Adams went back down to the kitchen.

"He needs ta rest," the old lady said, sounding concerned.

"My name is Jared, ma'am. Clay Jared."

"I'm Widow Simpson and this here is Miss Adams."

Claire looked at Jared. "What happened?"

"I know," Mrs. Simpson cut in. "It was a Box M cowboy who did it. Right?"

Jared nodded. "Two ganged up on him."

"An' you jumped in?"

"Yes."

"Well, that's somethin' ya don't see much of around here lately. A man who'll stand up ta the Box M."

Jared shrugged.

Claire stared at Jared, sizing him up. She made a decision.

"If you'll take us on to the Circle C, I'll pay you, Mr. Jared."

Jared shrugged. "Sure, ma'am. I got no place to be right now. I'm looking for a job anyway."

"Go down ta the stockyard office in the morning," the widow said. "Grab a chit fer the Circle C. They're hirin' an' they sure could use a man with iron balls!" She added, "Pardon my French!"

"Thanks, ma'am, I will," Jared chuckled. Claire Adams gave him a quick, embarrassed glance. She also stifled a giggle.

Mrs. Simpson made coffee and served apple-rhubarb tart to her guests. After that, Jared took his horse down to the barn and tended to its needs. It was getting dark so he curled up in a stall in a pile of straw with his saddle for a pillow and a blanket for a cover.

In the morning he had breakfast at a beanery then checked on Bob Marsh. He was much improved. He thanked Jared for helping him. Jared left to ride over to the stockyard and checked out the hiring board. It seemed there were only two outfits taking on help, the Circle C and the Box M.

"What's up?" Jared asked the clerk behind the cashier's cage. "How come there's only these two outfits hiring?"

The clerk snickered.

"What's so funny?" Jared asked.

"There were more, once, but the Circle C and the Box M cut the others out. Now all we got is them two giants staring each other down."

Jared thought about Slade and Turell.

"Yeah, I noticed."

"Last night they both had a shootout at the Black Bull Saloon. Did you hear about that?"

"No, I didn't," Jared lied.

"Well, two Box M men got killed. There's going to be hell to pay for that. You can bet on it."

"What's the law situation like here in town?"

The clerk snickered again.

"All we got is an old man hired to arrest drunks and clean up the horseshit from the streets for twenty dollars a month. That's about the extent of the law here, mister."

"Who buries the bodies?"

"That's left up to the Circle C and the Box M."

"I see," Jared replied.

"Yeah, it's a mess, alright," the clerk said.

Jared grabbed a Circle C chit from the board, stuck it in his shirt pocket and rode back across town to the bed and breakfast. Bob Marsh was sitting at the table drinking coffee.

"We're gonna leave in the morning, Jared," Marsh said. "It's been a privilege ta know ya."

"You ain't getting rid of me that easy, kid," Jared chuckled. He showed Marsh the Circle C chit.

The girls came down from upstairs. Celia Grant sat next to the young cowboy and put a hand on his forehead.

"No temperature," she said with authority.

"Are you sure, Miss Celia? Do it agin, please," Marsh was enjoying himself.

"We're leaving in the morning, Mr. Jared," Claire said. "Will you go with us?"

"Sure," Jared said.

He had a feeling that these two city girls had no idea what a mess awaited them at the Circle C.

7.

Jared came up from the barn ready to travel. Mrs. Simpson served them a breakfast with grits, ham, eggs and coffee and then they loaded the women's luggage into the back of the buckboard.

Later, Claire and Celia came down from their room dressed in their riding habits, looking very elegant in their jodhpurs, boots, vests and cowboy hats.

Marsh stared, wide-eyed. "You look real nice, Miss Celia."

"Why, thank you, Bob."

Celia Grant made room for the wounded cowboy to lay on a blanket among the luggage, using his saddle for a pillow.

"This is real neat, Miss Celia," Marsh said.

Jared helped Marsh up. After he got into a comfortable position, Celia Grant climbed in next to him.

"I have to take care of my patient," the girl said very seriously. "He is badly injured."

Jared tied Marsh's horse and his own to the tail of the buckboard and then climbed aboard. Claire climbed up on the buckboard bench beside him. He glanced over at her.

"It was a smart move, getting rid of that dress, ma'am."

"Thank you, Mr. Jared."

It was mid-morning of a warm, spring day when Jared flicked the reins and the buckboard moved at a slow pace. In half an hour, Fogelsburg disappeared behind them. Strange looking birds began to fly across the trail in front of them.

"What are they?" Claire asked.

"Road runners," Jared said.

Claire smiled and nodded, looking ahead at the far horizon.

"Everything is so wide open here," she remarked. "So big. It's not crowded like New York City."

"Is that where you're from, ma'am?"

"Yes. I'm a concert pianist, Mr. Jared."

"Really?" Jared sounded impressed.

"Yes. Do you like music?"

"Sure, but my music is different from your music."

"I see," Claire said but really didn't know what he meant.

"Are you going to play for the cows?" Jared chuckled.

Claire smiled. "That's very funny, Mr. Jared, very funny." A moment later, after visualizing it, she laughed also. "I see you have a sense of humor, Mr. Jared."

"We sing to them," Jared went on. "Sometimes we play the harmonica."

"Do cows like that?"

"Most times they do, yes. It calms them down. A good Irish tenor is worth his weight in gold on a cattle drive," Jared said. Claire laughed.

"Is that funny?" Jared asked.

"No, no! I was just thinking. Someone said that music soothes the savage beast. Have you heard that?"

"No, ma'am, I haven't, but I guess it's true."

They rode along in silence for a while. Claire turned to look back at Celia and Bob Marsh.

"How's the patient doing, Celia, dear?"

"He's sleeping soundly," she replied.

"Wonderful," Claire said.

A few moments later, Jared asked her, "Do you ride or shoot?"

Claire laughed again. "Mr. Compton's mother asked me that very same thing a few days ago. No, I have never ridden a horse nor shot a pistol, Mr. Jared."

Jared nodded. About three miles on he pulled the buckboard off the road and over into the shade of some aspens.

"Why are we stopping?"

Jared climbed down.

"You're going to break in your fancy riding clothes."

"I can't ride, Mr. Jared. I don't know how."

Jared untied his horse from the back of the buckboard and walked it around near the front. Claire was already standing there waiting, her eyes wide in expectation. She stroked the horse's neck.

"He's very handsome," she said.

The horse turned its head and sniffed her shoulder. She laughed softly.

"He's really a handsome animal."

"And he knows it," Jared said. "He already likes you." He adjusted the stirrups.

Celia climbed down to watch.

Jared went on. "Always mount from the left side," he explained. "Grab the saddle horn, put your left foot in the stirrup and swing up and over."

He talked Claire through the motions. When she was up in the saddle, he handed her the reins.

"We'll just go for a little walk." Jared held onto the hackamore, led the horse out into a wide field and stopped.

"How are you doing up there? How does it feel?"

"Just fine, I think, Mr. Jared." Claire said cautiously.

"Good. Listen to me, now," Jared said. "You have to remember what I say. When you want him to walk, just press both of your knees against his shoulders. If you want him to run then tap both of your heels against his barrel, here." Jared pointed. "If you want him to stop, pull the reins back. Okay?"

"Okay. I think so," Claire said. Her voice trembled.

"To turn him to the left, pull the reins to the left. For the right, pull them to the right. Okay?"

Claire nodded.

"Don't be scared. The horse will smell it. It'll confuse him."

"Alright. I'm fine. He's fine. We're both fine."

"Good. Keep that thought," Jared said as he stepped away from the horse. "Take him for a walk. He'll like that."

Bob Marsh sat in the back of the buckboard, watching. Celia stood close by.

Claire pressed her knees against the horse and it walked slowly out into the sunlit field. When they were about twenty yards away, she tapped the animal's barrel with her boot heels. The horse started off at a modest trot. They trotted to the end of the field, then out of sight.

"Oh, God," Celia cried, "she'll never find her way back!"

It was a half hour before they saw a tiny dot moving towards them across the field. It grew larger and came faster. In a few minutes, Claire Adams came galloping up. She brought the horse to a clean stop. Her face was flushed with excitement and she was breathing hard.

"He's wonderful! I just love him!" she cried.

"Dismount on the left," Jared said. "Always the left."

Claire dismounted. "Teach Celia!" she cried.

"Sure," Jared said. "If she wants to."

"No, not me!" Celia groaned.

"Yes, you will, you coward!" Claire insisted.

An hour later Celia Grant had taken her first ride on a horse. She was ecstatic. After dismounting, she hugged Bob Marsh and kissed him. Jared and Claire looked at each other and shared a laugh.

Celia Grant suddenly became very brave.

"Teach us to shoot," she said.

"Now, Celia, calm down," Claire told her friend. "We don't have time to play around."

"Sure we do, ma'am," Bob Marsh said. "We got plenty a time."

"Sure," Jared said. He turned to Claire. "Relax, Miss Adams. You're not in the city. We don't like to rush things here. Not unless we have to."

Claire sighed and smiled. "Alright, then."

After tying the horse to the buckboard, Jared placed a rock on top of a tree stump a few yards away.

He took Claire first.

"What you have to do," Jared said, taking out his Colt and holding it down at his right side, "is hold the gun down like this, then pull back the hammer as you raise it up to the rock. Once you got it pointing at the rock, you pull the trigger. Make sure you pull the hammer all the way back until it stays back. I'll do one."

Jared went through the motions again and shot at the rock, nicking a piece of it. The loud blast from the Colt made the girls flinch and hold their ears.

"It's really loud," Claire said.

"You'll get used to it," Jared replied. "Try to ignore it."

"Alright."

Jared spent an hour teaching both girls how to shoot.

After that, they moved the buckboard into a stand of pine trees where a stream ran fast and clear. They drank and sat in the cool shade of the pines. Bob Marsh got beef jerky and hardtack from his saddlebag and gave a piece of each to the girls.

"What's this?" Celia asked.

"Food, Miss Celia," Marsh replied.

The girl stared at it with a sour look on her face.

"Cowboys really eat this?" Claire asked.

"We sure do, ma'am."

"It stinks!" Celia said. "It looks disgusting."

"It smells better if'n yer really hungry, Miss Celia," Bob Marsh said. He bit off a piece of jerky and started chewing. "Go ahead, ma'am. Give it a try."

"Well, I am hungry," the girl from New York City muttered. She put the strip of dried meat to her mouth and took a small bite.

"Chew 'er good, Miss Celia," Bob advised.

Jared and Claire watched as the girl slowly chewed, expecting her to spit it out. But she didn't. Instead, she took another bite and finished it. She smiled proudly.

"Ma'am," Bob Marsh said happily, "yer a bona fide cowgirl now if there ever was one!"

"Try some, Claire," Celia Grant said. "It's really good." She turned to Marsh. "Hand me your canteen, Bob. I'm a little bit thirsty."

Marsh chuckled and handed her his canteen.

"Is this all you cowboys eat?" Claire asked, taking a bite of jerky.

"Shucks no, ma'am," Bob Marsh said. "Out on the drive we git ta eat steak and son of a gun stew."

"What in the world is that?" Celia asked. "It sounds awful!"

"It ain't so bad, dependin' on whose a cookin' it."

"What's in that stew, Mr. Marsh," Claire asked.

"Well, now, thet's a good question, ma'am," Marsh said. "It's mostly made of parts of a cow most people don't eat like the tongue, kidneys, heart and sech."

"You forgot the cow's brains, Bob," Jared added. "And the sweetbreads and tripe. It won't taste right without those."

"Oh, sure, pard," Marsh agreed. "Ya gotta have those."

"Yuck!" Celia cried out. "That sounds horrible!"

"Celia, dear, there is most likely no such thing as son of a gun stew. I've heard that cowboys are given to telling tall tales and stretching the truth."

Jared looked at Marsh and they both began laughing.

They went to the stream to refill the canteen and then got back on the road again. The sun was in the west and the trees threw long shadows. It grew cooler.

They reached the Circle C just before dark.

8.

Lorne Madison, a bull of a man, was tall and lean and had broad shoulders. He was also a handsome man with graying hair and fine features. When people saw him they took notice.

Madison owned the Box M Ranch. It was about the same size as the Circle C. In total, Madison's Box M and Compton's Circle C covered over 350,000 acres of grazing land and water sources. It was a lot of land, but their 150,000 head of cattle were pushing it to the limit.

Luckily, there was a dividing line called the Sandal River that separated their spreads. The mighty Sandal was kept alive and flowing by various streams that fed into it from both ranches.

Long ago, there had been dozens of small ranches in the Sandal Valley. Over time Compton and Madison gathered them up one by one, by hook or by crook. The end result was two hostile giants glaring at each other across the Sandal River, ready to strike at any time.

People in the outlying town of Fogelsburg wondered not if, but when these two monsters would go at each other's throats in an all-out range war. Almost weekly their cowboys drank, fought and died outside the Black Bull Saloon.

When this happened, as it so often did, the town marshal, old Tom Waverly, was left to toss the bodies in the back of a buckboard and haul them off to the Circle C and the Box M. There just wasn't enough room in the town cemetery for the locals, let alone the cowboys.

So when Marshal Waverly rode into the yard of the Box M, it was to deliver the bodies of Slade and Turell, two of Lorne Madison's best men. He knew Madison would be spitting mad.

"Here's two more, Lorne," the marshal said.

Madison walked to the back of the buckboard and pulled the canvas back to get a look at the bodies. Several cowboys came up from the barn to see who they were. Another few came from the bunkhouse. They knew why the marshal was there.

"Slade and Turell," Madison muttered. He didn't even ask who did the killing. It had to be the Circle C. There was no one else.

"Wrap 'em an' bury 'em, boys!" At a wave of Madison's hand, the cowboys lifted the bodies out of the buckboard and carried them into the bunkhouse to be wrapped in their bunk blankets.

Madison had stopped building caskets anymore.

"Look, Lorne," the marshal said from his seat on the buckboard, "I know what yer a thinkin'. Thet the Circle C provoked the fight. Well, it weren't thet way."

Madison stood staring off across the yard as if he wasn't interested in facts.

The marshal went on. "As I heard it, Slade an' Turell braced young Bob Marsh. It was two on one when a stranger stepped in ta even it up. As it was, Slade wounded the kid pretty bad."

Madison suddenly turned and glared at the marshal.

"What stranger?"

"Nobody knows who he was, but he was last seen drivin' a buckboard with Marsh an' two women on the old coach road, headin' fer the Circle C, I suspect."

"Two women? Out to the Circle C?"

"Yeah. Ol' Widow Simpson said they come from Kansas City ta visit the Circle C fer a spell, then head east."

Madison chuckled. "They must be special or plain stupid. Ardis Compton will eat them alive."

The two men fell silent for a moment listening to a dog barking down behind the barn.

The marshal finally broke the silence. "Well, Lorne, I'll be seein' ya."

Madison nodded and stepped aside as the marshal turned the buckboard and headed back for Fogelsburg. He stared after it for a while then sighed and went into the ranch house and into his study.

The house was very quiet and lonely. Madison listened to the sounds of the house for a moment then got a Bible out of a drawer and went outside again.

He walked down behind the bunkhouse and up to the plot where they buried all the cowboys. The two holes were already being dug. There were already fifteen wooden crosses.

Madison's short, stocky, sinister looking ramrod, Snake Norton, came over to him. His deep-set, coal black eyes blazed like smoldering embers under the brim of his hat. He fingered his gun with nervous energy.

"We can't let this go unanswered, Boss." Norton hissed like a snake. "Not Slade and Turell. They were the best we had."

"We won't," Madison replied.

"It's got ta be one fer one."

"Two fer one is better," the rancher said.

"Yeah, two fer one," Norton growled.

After the bodies were dropped in and the graves filled, Lorne Madison read from the Holy Bible. Then he went back to his big ranch house and thought about Ardis Compton.

9.

Lee Compton saw the buckboard ride into the yard and ran out to greet it. When he saw Celia Grant in the back with Bob Marsh he knew something had happened, but he went straight to Claire and helped her down.

"It's good to see you again, Claire." Compton kissed her on the cheek and took her hand in his.

"And you, Lee." Claire returned the kiss.

The rancher noticed the stranger in the driver's seat and stared at him for a moment, then turned back to Bob Marsh and Celia.

"What happened, Marsh?"

"He's been shot," Celia said before the cowboy could answer.

"Shot?" Compton turned back to Claire. "Were you attacked on the road?" He turned his gaze quickly to Jared. "I don't believe I know you, sir."

Bob Marsh and Celia climbed out of the buckboard.

"He's a friend of mine, sir," Marsh said.

"Were you shot, Marsh?" He noticed the bloody shirt.

"Ah, yes I was, Mr. Compton."

"Where?"

"In Fogelsburg, sir."

Just then, Del Benton, the old, silver-haired ramrod, came limping over. He gave the young cowboy the once over.

"Who tagged ya, Bob?"

"Fig Turell," Marsh answered.

"Were ya in the Black Bull, kid?"

"Ah, well, sorta."

The thin, frail ramrod nodded. "I see." His stern look said more than words.

"I didn't start it," the young cowboy said.

"We'll settle thet later, kid," Benton said. He turned to scrutinize Jared who was still sitting on the buckboard seat. "Who are you, mister?"

Jared jumped down and held out his hand.

"Jared. Clay Jared."

"Never heard of you," Benton sneered. He left Jared's hand dangling.

"I hear you're hiring," Jared said as he handed Benton the Circle C chit.

"Maybe, maybe not," Benton said.

"Come, ladies, Mother is waiting!"

Lee Compton took Claire's hand and led her and Celia towards the huge ranch house.

Del Benton turned and pointed to two cowboys of the several who had gathered around.

"Take the bags up ta the house, boys. The rest of you git back ta doin' what ya were a-doin'."

The cowboys scattered, leaving Benton facing Jared and Marsh.

"Okay, kid, spit it out!"

"I felt like a drink so I went up ta the Black Bull. Whilst I was there, Slade and Turell began messin' with me. I kinda lost my temper."

"How did ya git tagged?"

"Slade braced me and Turell looked like he was in, too."

Jared cut in. "They were setting the kid up for a clean kill. I saw it coming so I stepped in."

"So, it turned out you got shot by Slade. You're lucky ta be alive, Marsh."

"Yeah, I'm lucky, but they ain't."

"What's thet suppose ta mean?"

"Slade and Turell ain't gonna kill no more Circle C boys ever agin. Thet's what it means."

"You two took Slade and Turell out?"

"Sorta, kinda, hell yeah! We sure as heck did."

The old ramrod whistled.

"You joshin' me, kid?"

"Nope. Jest you ask my pard here. He'll tell ya."

"Is it true, Jared?" Jared nodded. "Christ! I'll have ta tell Mr. Compton."

"You gonna punish me, Boss?" the young cowboy asked.

"Maybe. I ain't figured it out yet."

"What about me?" Jared asked. "Hire me or let me move on."

"Where'd ya wrangle before?"

"Flying J, Diamond S and the Lazy W were the last three."

"You sure move around a lot, mister." Jared shrugged. The old man studied Jared for a moment, trying to puzzle him out. He scratched his jaw. "Okay. I'll take ya on fer a month. After thet we'll see."

Jared chuckled. "One month?"

"Yep. Take it 'er leave it, Jared."

"Hell, why not. I'm in no hurry. It won't hurt me to waste a month."

Benton looked at Bob Marsh.

"Kid, I'm gonna send ya out to the east line shack fer a while jest ta keep ya out of trouble."

"Oh, no!" Marsh was crushed.

"Leave tamorry. An' tell Sanders ta stay with ya."

Bob Marsh saw Celia Grant slipping through his fingers.

"Heck, Boss, I ain't in no shape ta ride out there. I been wounded bad."

"Alright. I'll give ya two days light duty helpin' the cook," Benton said. "An' stay clear of the women."

The old ramrod walked away towards the barn smiling inside himself. He really liked the kid. He had stood up for the Circle C and Benton admired that. And as for this new man, Jared, they could use an extra fast gun on the spread.

Things were going to get pretty darn messy soon.

10.

It was a fine, simple meal, roast chicken with pole beans and mashed potatoes and gravy, followed by baked raisin bread pudding covered in caramel sauce. It was made and served by Mrs. Tully, who also did the cleaning. She was a widow and lived in a room off the larder.

They topped the meal off with a bottle of claret Lee Compton had brought back from Kansas City.

Ardis Compton sat at the head of the table facing her son at the other end. Claire and Celia sat facing each other in the middle.

"Miss Adams, did Lee tell you about his travels in Europe?" Mrs. Compton asked.

"No, Mrs. Compton, he has not," Claire said, smiling up the table at Lee.

"Oh, Lee is a well-traveled man," Mrs. Compton went on. "He spent a year at Oxford as a guest student. Yes, I saw to it that Lee had a liberal education even though his father had other plans for him."

"Now, Mother, the girls don't want to hear about my education, I'm sure."

Ardis Compton gave Claire a patronizing stare.

"I suppose you're well educated, are you not, Miss Adams?"

"Actually most of my education has been in the musical field, ma'am. I studied at a small school for gifted children in New York. I'm afraid it's not as famous as Oxford."

"Lee also attended Princeton."

"How commendable." Claire smiled at Lee Compton again.

"Mother is always bragging about me when we have guests," he said. "It embarrasses me."

Ardis Compton turned her eyes to Celia. "And you, Miss Grant. What college did you attend?"

Celia suddenly felt uncomfortable and cornered.

"Ah, well, ma'am, I grew up with Claire. We attended the same public schools together. We're sorta like sisters."

"Oh? How do you support yourself, Miss Grant? Surely you have an occupation."

Claire quickly cut into the conversation. "Celia is my companion."

'I see. Then I take it you support her, do you?"

"I pay her salary, yes," Claire said flatly. She didn't care for the intrusive questions.

"What happens to Miss Grant if and when you decide to marry, Miss Adams? Will Miss Grant share---"

There was a sudden embarrassing silence. Celia's face was flushed.

"Mother!" Lee Compton cried. He turned to Celia Grant. "Please forgive my mother, Celia. She's had a little too much wine to drink, I suspect."

"Yes," Ardis Compton said, "perhaps I have." She took another sip of claret. "What do your parents do for a living, Miss Adams?"

"My father is a lawyer in New York. My mother, well, she supports local charities, mostly."

"Oh, how nice," Ardis said dryly. "A lawyer. We have several of those in Kansas City. A dishonest lot, at best."

"Mother! That's enough!" Lee Compton yelled.

Claire looked at Ardis Compton and smiled.

"Mrs. Compton," she said in a calm, sympathetic tone of voice. "Your son invited Celia and me here as temporary guests. I am not his fiancé nor are we in a relationship of that nature."

"Then why did you accept his offer if you're not interested in him? Do you accept every strange man's offer?"

"No, ma'am, I do not!"

"Then why did you accept his?"

"Well, I…"

"Yes?"

"I had just finished up my concert tour and was planning to take a month off and relax. Tours are difficult, with all the traveling and stress, you know."

"No, I do not know."

"And Celia wanted to see what the West was like. So when your son was gracious enough to ask us to be his guests, we accepted. He seemed like a sincere and honest man, and I know he is a gentleman."

This seemed to take the wind out of Ardis Compton.

"You'll have to forgive my mother," Lee Compton said. "She's a bit overprotective of me. I'm sure you understand,"

"Yes," Claire said. "I'm convinced she is."

Lee smiled down the length of the table at his mother.

"And, Mother," he said cheerfully, "I had a motive for inviting Miss Adams to our home." He stood up. "Come, Claire!"

Claire stood up and took Compton's outstretched hand. He led her into the great room to a concert grand piano near the fireplace.

"My father had this brought in from St. Louis," Lee said. "It has held its tune well. I like to play songs for Mother on occasion, but I'm afraid I don't play very well. It comes in handy around Christmas time when we sing carols."

Claire noticed a pile of sheet music on a small table by the piano. She looked through it, selecting a few.

"Do you sing, Lee?"

"I do try, Claire."

Ardis Compton and Celia took chairs near the fireplace. Claire sat down at the piano and opened the keyboard lid.

"Let's try, 'The Last Rose of Summer,'" Claire suggested, opening the sheet music.

"Alright."

It went well. Lee Compton had a deep, rich bass. He went on to sing "Coming Through the Rye", "Believe Me If All Those Endearing Young Charms", and, "Long, Long Ago".

Finally, Lee asked Claire to play "Liebestraum" and "Träumerei".

The soothing music calmed the volatile Ardis Compton down and she dozed off into dreamland.

Down at the bunkhouse the cowboys stopped talking over the card table and listened. They were pleased.

"I'll be danged! They finally got somebody thet kin tame thet black mustang!" one of them snorted.

11.

Snake Norton, ramrod of the Box M, was not happy. Two of his best men had been shot down like dogs outside the Black Bull Saloon in Fogelsburg by a snot-nosed kid from the Circle C and a meddling drifter from nowhere. Now his boss expected him to do something about it.

Norton was a careful man. As ramrod of the Box M for five years now, he had handled crisis after crisis with skilled hands, striking at its enemies when and where they least expected it. That was why they called him Snake.

The night after the shootout in Fogelsburg, Norton gathered his cowboys together in the bunkhouse by the light of an oil lamp.

"Men," he said, "we got us a situation here. Slade an' Turell are six feet under and the skunk thet done it is over at the Circle C playin' poker like nothin' happened."

"We should ventilate the son of a bitch!" Edge Cole, Norton's assistant ramrod, said.

"Yeah," someone replied. "Hang the bastard!"

"His name is Bob Marsh," Norton said. "He musta got real lucky ta have beat Slade or Turell ta the draw."

"He's only part of the problem," someone replied. "Compton is pushin' his cattle further east across the Sandal."

"We ought ta push 'em right back inta Compton's face!" another cowboy suggested.

"Hell no! We ought ta grab 'em all up! Rebrand 'em 'an keep 'em, I say."

"Yeah," another said. "Or better yet, sell 'em over the county line. There's plenty buyers out there. We could make a bundle."

"We'll keep 'em," Norton said. "Madison has declared every cow east of the Sandal belongs ta the Box M. We'll rebrand 'em, an' thet's all there is to thet."

"Maybe Compton doesn't know what's a-goin' on," one cowboy commented.

"Well, in a few days he'll know right well enough," Edge Cole replied. "Right, Snake?"

Norton nodded. He rolled a cigarette, taking his time. Finally, he lit it over the oil lamp and blew a cloud of smoke up at the ceiling.

"He sure will," Norton finally replied smugly.

"There's two women over there now," a cowboy named Fern Bailey said. "Three, countin' the ol' lady."

"So what?" Edge Cole sneered. "What's yer point, Bailey?"

Bailey shrunk back into the group. "Nothin'. I'm jest a sayin' is all."

"Well, shut up about it!" Cole growled.

"Sure," Baily muttered.

Norton's narrowed eyes swept over the group of a dozen or more cowboys.

"Douglas, Thomas, Ederly," he said. "In my room, now. The rest of you jokers go back ta playin' grab ass."

The three men stood up and followed Norton and Cole into the back room of the bunkhouse. A bottle of whiskey sat next to an oil lamp on a wooden table with four chairs. Norton stood while the rest sat down.

"Mr. Madison wants some action, boys, an' I aim ta give him some," Norton said.

Cole pulled the cork on the bottle and handed it to Douglas who took a pull and passed it on to Thomas.

"So what I'm gonna do is appoint you three and Cole as Regulators."

"Like in the ol' days?" Thomas asked. He took the bottle from Douglas and took a nip.

"Thet's right. In the ol' days when the people seen somethin' needed fixin', they fixed it themselves."

"What about the law?" Thomas asked.

"The Regulators was the law, asshole," Edge Cole shot back.

"So, whatta we gonna do, Snake?" Douglas asked.

"Fer starters, we're gonna take out the Circle C's east end line shack," Norton answered.

"What about the cowpokes? They'll fight back won't they?" Ederly said.

"They'll run like scared rabbits," Cole snickered. "They ain't got the backbone ta fight back."

"What if they do? Won't that start a war?" Ederly wouldn't drop it. He seemed on edge.

"Maybe thet's what we need," Snake Norton growled. "The Sandal Valley ain't big enough fer Compton and us. Somebody has ta pull back an' it sure as hell ain't gonna be the Box M."

The all nodded except young Ederly.

12.

Celia Grant sat on the porch steps of the Circle C Ranch house trying to concentrate on the letter she was writing to her parents back in New York City. The fact that it was a warm and vibrant spring day made it difficult.

So far she had written:

Dear Mom and Dad,

I hope this letter finds you both well and happy. As for me, I'm having a wonderful time. Claire and I are guests of rancher Lee Compton and his mother on the Circle C Ranch.

It is amazing how everything is so open here in Kansas. It is a grand land so big it takes your breath away. It takes days to go from one end of the ranch to the other.

I'm sitting here on the porch looking down at the corral watching the cowboys mounting up and going out on the range. They look so noble on their fine horses with their lariats hanging from their saddle horns. (I'm learning to speak cowboy! They say colorful words like 'shucks,' and 'dang it all' and 'thet's fer sure'.)

They ride out with guns in holsters and rifles in sheaths and spend weeks tending to the cattle and sleeping under the stars. And the cattle? My God!

The herds are enormous and stretch into the distance and beyond.

Claire is also having a grand time. I think Mr. Compton has an eye for her. He is the perfect western gentleman. I'm sure he would have asked her to be engaged if it wasn't for his mother, who is somewhat difficult to deal with.

There's talk of a conflict going on between the Circle C and the ranch next door, the Box M.

The girl stopped writing for a moment, wondering if she should tell her parents about Bob Marsh being wounded in a gunfight with two Box M men in Fogelsburg. She didn't want to worry them, so she didn't.

Instead, she wrote:

I have met some very interesting cowboys here. Men like Mr. Jared who taught Claire and me how to ride a horse and shoot a pistol. He's a real cowboy. And there is also a fine young cowboy named Bob Marsh who picked us up in Ellsworth in a buckboard. Mr. Marsh has a picture book about Vikings that he just loves. He's much taken with them, especially the way they are buried. It fascinates him.

Celia stopped writing a moment to stare at a cat walking across the yard with a mouse in its mouth. It strolled down towards the barn, out of sight.

She was about to begin writing again when she saw Bob Marsh walking his horse up from the barn. It was all saddled up with a bedroll and saddlebags. Celia put her writing tablet and pencil aside and stood up.

"Hello, Bob."

"Howdy, Miss Celia," Bob said "I jest came ta say adios, ma'am." He stopped in front of her.

"Adios? That sounds so permanent, Bob. Why not just say, see ya later?"

"Alright then, Miss Celia, I'll see ya later."

"Where are you going?"

"Up to the east line shack fer a spell."

"How long will that be?"

"A couple of weeks, most likely, ma'am."

The young girl from New York City stood looking up into the cowboy's eyes. He stared helplessly back.

"I'll miss you, Bob. Very much," Celia said softly.

"I'll sure as heck miss you, too, Miss Celia."

"I may be gone by the time you return, Bob."

"Yes ma'am, I reckon thet's true." The tall, lean cowboy looked away for a moment. A breeze tugged at his red bandana and hat. "Kin I ask ya fer a favor?"

"Yes, Bob, you can."

"Ah, ya think you could maybe give me a token?"

"A token?"

"Yes, ma'am. Somethin' ta remember ya by, after yer gone."

"What would you like?"

"I heard about where the ladies use ta give their knights a token when they won a fight."

Celia nodded. "Alright. Wait a minute. I'll get one."

The girl went into the house and came out a few minutes later with a delicate, pink, perfume scented handkerchief.

"Will this do?" she said, handing it to the cowboy.

"Yes, ma'am. It sure will." Bob Marsh chuckled and smiled. He held it to his nose and inhaled, then carefully put it in his shirt pocket.

They stood looking into each other's eyes. Neither one knew what else to do. Finally, the cowboy touched the brim of his hat in a goodbye salute.

"Adios, Miss Celia."

"Goodbye, cowboy."

Bob Marsh swung up into the saddle and rode slowly out of the yard of the Circle C. In a few minutes he'd ridden up and over a rise in the road. Suddenly he was gone.

Celia Grant sat on the porch steps and began writing again.

Bob Marsh just came by to say goodbye. He's going out on range duty and will be gone for a few weeks. He's such a fine young cowboy. I just love him so.

She stared down at the last sentence and thought about erasing it, but didn't.

Suddenly the yard of the Circle C seemed very empty.

13.

A few days after Bob Marsh left for the east line shack, Lee Compton called his ramrod, Del Benton, into his study in the ranch house. Compton was at his desk going over some papers when Benton came in.

"Ya wanted ta see me, Mr. Compton, sir?"

"Did you send Bob Marsh up to the east line shack, Del?"

"Yes, sir."

"I thought he was wounded and couldn't work."

"Yes, sir," Benton replied. "I sent him up there ta take it easy. Fuzzy Sanders is there already. Marsh kin keep him company."

"I see." Compton shifted some papers around.

"Is thet it, sir?"

"Ah, not really, Del. There's one more thing. Miss Adams and Miss Grant would like to go up there. I told them you'd give them a tour of the place."

The old ramrod scratched his head. "The east line shack?" He sounded surprised.

"Yes. It's only half a day's ride, isn't it?"

"Yes, sir, fer a cowpoke it is. But fer them ladies it'll take a mite longer, I suspect."

"Take whatever supplies you need for their comfort," Compton said, looking at a folder of paperwork.

His mind was clearly on more important matters.

"It'll most likely be an overnight stay, sir."

"I will tell them that, Del, but it won't change their minds. They seem to have some silly romantic notion of how things are out here in the West."

"Most tenderfoots do, Boss."

"Take someone reliable with you, just in case," Compton said. "And you'll have to let the women have the shack to themselves. So take extra blankets for sleeping outside."

Del Benton nodded. He didn't like the whole matter much but there wasn't anything he could do to change things.

"That's all, Del." Compton went back to his paperwork.

Back in the bunkhouse the ramrod cornered Tom Andrews, his second in command, and explained the situation.

"So, you'll be in charge until I git back, Tom."

Del Benton looked around the bunkhouse. He spotted Jared lying on his bunk.

"You!" he said, pointing a finger at Jared.

Jared sat up. "Me?"

"Yeah, you, mister. Yer goin' with me."

Jared shrugged. "Okay, Boss."

"We'll be needin' a few extra blankets for the women."

"What about food?"

"They'll have one meal of jerky and hardtack. That'll have ta hold 'em until we git ta the shack. There's plenty of food there. We'll need extra canteens, though."

"When are we leaving?"

"In the morning, as soon as they're ready."

Jared nodded. Actually he was pleased. He had been hoping to see Claire Adams again and now he would be close to her for a day or two.

The two men got up an hour before breakfast and saddled up two horses for the girls. They tied a bedroll behind each saddle and put a canteen of fresh water in the saddlebags with some jerky and hardtack.

They had breakfast and waited under the lean-to by the cook's outfit next to the bunkhouse. When the girls came out of the house, they walked all the horses up to them and mounted. It was almost mid-morning when the little caravan followed Del Benton out onto the road.

It had been a week now and the women's riding skills had much improved. Claire and Celia rode side by side with Jared bringing up the rear.

Ten miles to the east they came to the Sandal River and turned left, following it northward. Its clear water flowed rapidly south over bedrock, making it sparkle like diamonds in the sunlight. It was a river worth fighting for, clear and pure.

In some places, cat o' nine tails and tiger lilies grew in abundance along the river edge. They saw deer drinking on the far side. Eagles circled overhead.

The girls gazed about them as if in a dream.

They came to a high rock outcropping and had to turn west away from the Sandal. A few miles on and they picked up the trail again. It led them northwest and it ran through a forest of tall pines. The winds whispered aloft.

They stopped by a clear, fast flowing stream and dismounted to rest and let the horses nibble grass and drink. They sat nearby and ate.

"How much more?" Jared asked.

"Another three hours should do it," the old ramrod said.

Claire and Celia got up and walked to the stream.

"There's fish in there!" Celia yelled.

"Trout," Benton chuckled. "Best eatin' in the world. Some weigh near five pounds."

In half an hour they saddled up again and went on.

They were in some trees not far from the line shack when they heard the sound of gunfire.

Benton looked at Jared.

"Thet don't sound good."

"What's wrong?" Claire asked Benton.

"Somethin' is goin' on up at the shack," Benton replied.

They rode closer to the sound, staying in the pines. Finally, they came to a narrow field of prairie grass and then to a rise. They stopped again.

"Stay here with the women," Benton said. "I'm gonna take a gander."

The old ramrod dismounted, pulled his Winchester from its sheath and walked slowly over the rise and out of sight. A few moments later they heard Benton's rifle bark twice.

Jared jumped down and grabbed his rifle. He turned to Claire. "Stay here. Don't dismount. If you see anyone, ride back into the trees and hide there."

Jared crouched down and ran up and over the rise. On the other side, he saw old Del Benton flat on his belly behind a big rock. He crawled up next to him and looked ahead.

Shooters were pouring round after round into the line shack. No one inside seemed to be firing back. The windows were all shot out and the front of the structure was riddled with bullet holes. The attackers were well hidden behind boulders. Only the barrels of their rifles were visible.

"Looks like four of 'em," Benton said.

"Yeah, I think you're right."

The old man took careful aim and fired, hitting the edge of a boulder fifty feet away. Someone screamed in pain.

"I sure put rock dust in thet bushwhacker's face!" Benton chuckled.

Jared followed suit and levered three shots into the boulders, sending rock shards flying in all directions.

"Let's vamoose!" someone down below yelled.

The firing stopped, the rifle barrels pulled back and moments later they heard horses moving in the pine trees behind the rocks.

"They're pullin' out," Benton yelled.

The old man and Jared stood up slowly, holding their rifles at the ready. They waited a while until the sound of the horses faded, then walked down to the bunkhouse. What they saw made them gasp. The entire front of the line shack had been blasted to shreds.

"Lordy, lordy!" the old ramrod whined. He stared at the bullet holes in disbelief. "I can't go in there!"

Suddenly they heard a groan inside the shack. Jared quickly opened the door and rushed in. Benton came behind him.

Ben Marsh and Fuzzy Sanders lay in a pool of blood, their bodies riddled with bullets. Sanders was plainly dead with a bullet hole between his eyes. Marsh tried to raise a hand but let it fall on his chest. Jared knelt at his side and started to lift him up.

"Don't," the young cowboy said. His voice was less than a whisper. "It hurts too much, pard."

"Who were they, kid?" Benton asked.

"Cole and..."

"Who's Cole?" Jared asked.

"He's Snake Norton's gunny," Benton replied. "This was done by the Box M boys. Damn them ta hell!"

"We can't be sure unless we find them," Jared said.

Just then, they heard a scream back behind the rise.

"The women!" Benton yelled.

"Save Celia," Bob Marsh whispered. Blood bubbled from the corner of his mouth.

Jared and the old man rushed out of the shack and up the hill. When they reached the top Jared saw two men grabbing the reins away from the girls. The other two fired shots at them.

"They got the girls!" Benton screamed.

He and Jared scrambled behind a boulder and lay on the ground, listening to the thunder of horses fading in the distance. When they got back to the top of the rise again, they saw their horses were gone, too.

14.

"Whatta we gonna do now?" the old man asked. "We got no horses and they're gettin' clean away!"

"You go back to the shack and take care of the kid," Jared said. He stood up and started walking away.

"Where the hell ya goin'?"

"I'm gonna track them down."

Benton watched as Jared crouched over and began running like an Indian, balancing the weight of his Winchester in his right hand. He was soon deep into the pine forest.

The old man turned and rushed back down the rise into the shack and knelt by Bob Marsh's side.

"I'm a goner, Del," Marsh whispered. "Give me a Vikin's send off, won't ya, Boss?"

"Sure, kid. I'll give ya one, if thet's what ya want."

The young cowboy tried to talk but coughed up blood instead.

The old man knew the kid was going fast now. He took his hand and held it until Bob Marsh let out a long, soft sigh.

"Goodbye, kid." The old ramrod said. His eyes were moist. He sniffed and wiped the wetness away. "I'm sorry I was mean ta ya. You were a damn good cowboy."

The old warrior tried to lift the young cowboy's body but couldn't, so he got behind it, grabbed it under the arms and dragged it over to a bunk. He levered it up and over until he had it all in and stretched out, face up. Finally, he put the kid's Colt in his hand, laying it across his chest.

The old ramrod looked over at the bullet-riddled body of Sanders. He went to it.

"Ya were a mean, lazy son of a bitch, Sanders," Benton sniffed. "Now yer gonna do some good."

The old ramrod strained and hauled away at Sanders' heavy carcass until he finally got it laid across the bunk at the feet of Bob Marsh.

"I can't find no pig, so Sanders will have ta do, kid."

The old man looked around, sighing. Everything in sight was full of bullet holes. The saddles and saddlebags were riddled, and the stocks of the Winchesters were splintered and broken. The frying pan that hung from a peg near the stove looked like a sieve. The stovepipe had taken over a dozen hits.

"Lord Almighty," Benton said out loud.

The place held the stench of death.

Benton grabbed Sanders' saddlebag, opened it and looked in. It had some jerky and hardtack wrapped in wax paper. He closed it and slung it over his shoulder then grabbed two canteens.

In the kid's saddlebag he found the child's picture book about Vikings that Marsh had always kept close. He tore some pages out of it, made a torch of them and lit it. He dropped it on the empty bunk next to Marsh and Sanders and waited until it flared up.

"So long, cowboys," Benton said softly, sniffing back tears.

He took one last look around and went outside, leaving the door open so that the wind could fan the flames inside. It wasn't long before the fire was shooting up through the roof.

Ten miles away, Jared struggled along. After running at a steady pace for the last eight miles he had to will each leg to move. They felt like they were made of lead. The air burned his lungs with each breath. He stopped to lean over, gasping as if drowning.

He heard the sound of running water up ahead and marched toward it. Once there, he collapsed on his knees and drank, then put his face into it to cool off.

Later he discovered horse tracks leading across the stream into a stand of birch trees. The trail was easy to follow in the soft earth. Climbing a rise, he stared back to see a large orange ball of fire in the distance where the east line shack was. He thought about it for a few moments then began running again.

15.

Several times Celia Grant saw a chance to grab the reins of her horse from the hands of the young cowboy Ederly and make a run for it. Each time she held back, afraid to leave Claire behind in the hands of the monster, Edge Cole. So instead, she just slipped from her saddle and sat on the ground, folding her arms like a stubborn child.

Her captors pulled their horses to a stop. Cole dismounted and walked back to her.

"Git up, bitch!"

"No, I am tired and hungry. And so is Claire."

"I said git up!"

"I will not!"

Cole reached down and grabbed the girl by the hair, then pulled her up on her feet and slapped her across the face. She grunted and moaned in pain.

"Ya didn't have ta do thet, Cole," young Ederly said.

Cole stared hard at Ederly. "Shut yer mouth, kid. This is my party, not yers!"

"Where we takin' 'em?" Thomas asked.

"Up ta thet old, abandoned mine," Cole answered. "There's a couple of deserted cabins there."

"An' then what?" Douglas asked.

"I'll have thet all figured out by the time we git there," Cole replied. "So don't worry about it."

Claire Adams cleared her throat. "I'll give ten thousand dollars to all of you if you let us go." Edge Cole turned to her with a skeptical look. He sneered.

"How the hell ya gonna do thet, huh?"

"Just take us to the closest telegraph station and I will wire my father to send an order to any bank you want."

Douglas and Thomas looked at each other with a smile. They had never seen close to that much money in their lives.

"Did you say ten thousand, lady?" Douglas asked.

"Yes, I did, sir," Claire responded.

Douglas turned to Edge Cole.

"What about it, Cole?"

"She's jest stallin' fer time is all," Cole growled. "There ain't no ten thousand dollars!"

He grabbed Celia Grant and swung her up into the saddle. He cut a length of rope from Ederly's lariat and tied her hands to the saddle horn. He then mounted up.

"Let's go, an' no more talk about ten thousand dollars, lady!"

Edge Cole took the lead and led them across the Sandal River at a shallow point then turned to follow it north.

"How far, Edge?" Thomas asked after an hour of riding around rocks and through pine stands.

"About an hour more," Cole replied. "Keep an eye on them two and stop askin' questions."

It was sundown when they rode across a small field of prairie grass and through an opening in a rock wall that led to the mining camp. It was at the side of a stream and much of its abandoned equipment lay discarded like dead bodies left to decay with time. Even the two shacks leaned sadly as if exhausted and ready to fall over.

After they dismounted, Cole took Douglas aside and spoke to him low.

"Douglas, you remember the shortcut back ta the Box M?"

"Sure, Boss."

"Good. I want you to ride fer the Box M and see Snake. Tell him we got the bait fer the trap up here at the mine. Ya got thet?"

"Sure, I got it, Boss," Douglas answered.

"An' tell him I said the rest is up ta him."

Douglas nodded and repeated, "The rest is up ta him."

Cole patted Douglas on the shoulder. The cowboy mounted up again and rode quickly away.

16.

Douglas rode fast and two hours later came pounding into the yard of the Box M. He went straight up to Snake Norton and told him about the women and how they wiped out the Circle C east line shack.

"Who was in it?" Norton asked.

Douglas chuckled sneered. "Thet asshole Fuzzy Sanders an' the kid, Bob Marsh."

Norton nodded, smiling. "Thet puts an' end ta thet little sidewinder, I reckon."

"It sure does, Boss. I wish Slade and Turell had a been there with us."

"So, Cole has the girls, does he?"

"Yeah," Douglas chuckled. "An' thet dark haired one, she tried ta bribe us."

Norton's eyes narrowed with interest. He stroked his chin.

"How much?"

"Ten thousand. She said her ol' man is a rich lawyer in New York and he'd wire the money to any bank we wanted."

Snake Norton nodded.

"Thet's somethin' ta keep in mind fer later, after this whole shindig is over. If they're alive, thet is."

"What?" Douglas asked.

"Nothin'," the big ramrod said. "Look, Douglas, we gotta move fast and finish this thing once and fer all. Git a small rock and meet me in the bunkhouse."

Norton went inside, got a piece of paper and wrote a note. It read:

If ya want ta see the wimin alive, come an' git 'em at the ol' mine camp. You'll have ta fight fer 'em so bring all the men ya got.

When Douglas returned with the rock, Norton got some twine and tied the note to it.

"Alright, Douglas, you rest up for a while," the ramrod said. Douglas nodded and went to lay on his bunk. Norton called over another cowboy and handed the rock to him.

"Tim, ride over ta the Circle R bunkhouse, throw this rock through the window and skedaddle back here."

Tim, like a good soldier, took the rock without asking any questions and left the bunkhouse. Snake Norton stood in the middle of the bunkhouse and gathered his troops around him.

"Gather around, men," he said loudly.

The cowboys assembled around their commander.

"Listen up, cowboys! It's time ta separate the men from the boys, the wolves from the rabbits, the brave from the yellah-bellies!"

Norton's men listened closely. They sensed this was an important matter.

"We're gonna have it out with the Circle C once an' fer all!"

The meaning of these last words quickly sank in. It was war, ugly and deadly, as all range wars were. Only the new cowboys didn't realize what that really meant.

"Is Mr. Madison in on it?" someone asked.

"He sure is," Norton said. "The Circle C has been poppin' our boys off fer a long time now, and it ain't gonna happen no more. Madison wants it stopped and so do I."

"Then, its war is it?"

"It is, plain an' simple," Norton admitted.

The bunkhouse became quiet. The cowboys looked at each other. Some were not happy. A range war always resulted in not only death but a change in their lives, too. They would lose friends. Perhaps the ranch would close down. Sometimes the law would step in. It could be a mess.

"Any yellah-bellies?" Norton asked, putting his hand down by his Colt.

"What's in it fer us?" one brave soul asked.

"Who said thet?" Norton growled. A cowboy stood up. He looked very scared. "Yer finished, Addison. Hit the trail."

"Don't I get my back pay?"

"If'n ya don't ride out right now, yer gonna get a bullet in yer yellah ass! An' thets all yer gonna git!"

Without another word the cowboy rolled up his blanket, grabbed his saddle and saddlebag from under his bunk and left.

Norton's face changed. He gave the cowboys a stern look.

"Anybody else wanna pull out?"

Nobody moved. Norton's face changed. He gave them a fatherly look and spoke calmly.

"Listen, men, when ya sign on ta ride fer the brand, yer obligated ta honor thet commitment. When ya ride fer the brand, ya ride fer the brand and it's a bond ya can't break. You all know thet. Ya can't pick an' chose when ta fight an' not ta fight. Yer in all the way, like it or not."

Norton let his words soak in for a while.

"Yer either a Box M cowboy or yer not. Which is it gonna be?"

For a moment, there was an uncertain silence. Then murmurs slowly started rippling like a wave on a still pond throughout the room. Suddenly one cowboy jumped up and clenched a fist.

"We're in, Boss! Damn right we are!"

A chorus of cheering burst out through the bunkhouse door into the night.

Snake Norton nodded in approval. He was now ready to strike.

17.

Clay Jared was just about to give up the chase when he heard horses in the woods behind him. Just as he turned and drew his Colt, Del Benton rode up with another horse in tow. It was his.

"They came back when things quieted down," Benton said. "Jesus! You look about ta croak."

"I feel like it, too," Jared replied, sitting on the ground, trying to fill his lungs with air. Benton tossed him a canteen.

"Thanks," Jared said, after taking a long pull of water. "What was going on back there?"

"I gave the kid a Viking send off," the old man said. "It's the least I could do fer him."

"That leaves one more thing."

"What's thet?"

"Plug the bastards who killed him and Sanders."

"That's fer sure. Thet's fer dang sure," Benton said. "Ya want ta rest a while?"

For an answer, Jared got slowly to his feet. After putting his Winchester back in its sheath, he grabbed the saddle horn of his horse and swung up into the saddle. He patted the horse's neck. The horse neighed.

"How fur ahead do ya reckon they are, Jared?"

"A long ways. And it's getting too dark to see the tracks anymore. Maybe we should wait here until morning."

"It'll be a full moon," Benton said, "and the trail is pretty clear. I've been this way a few times."

"Where does it lead?" Jared asked.

"There's a deserted mine up ahead. Maybe two hours. It's where I'd camp fer the night if'n I was them."

"Let's go, then."

They started out at a walk then moved faster as the moon rose in the night sky. Sometimes they had to slow down where the tracks went into the shadows of the trees. Finally, they came to the Sandal River.

"Looks like they crossed over here. Thet means they're a headin' fer the old mine," Benton said.

They crossed over and followed the tracks north.

They soon passed a rock outcropping that twisted and turned with the trail. Once across the field and through the trees, the old man pulled his horse to a stop.

"We'd best slow down to a walk, Jared, less they kin hear us. Sound carries fur in the night."

When they came to the opening in the rock wall, they dismounted and entered slowly on foot. Once inside, they tied their horses to some bushes and crouched down as they followed the stream up into the camp.

There were two men standing by a small fire. They were both drinking coffee. One bent over to pick up the pot to refill his cup.

"Thet's Thomas," Benton whispered to Jared. "The young un is Ederly. They ride fer the Box M."

"I don't see the girls," Jared whispered back.

"Most likely they're up in one of the cabins."

Just then, they heard Claire Adams's voice coming from one of the rundown shacks. She was arguing with a man. There was a loud slap and a groan. A man came out and over to the fire.

"Thet bitch keeps talkin' back," the man said.

Benton touched Jared on the shoulder. "Thet's Edge Cole," he said. "He's Snake Norton's best man. Fast as greased lightnin' on the draw."

"Then I'll take him first," Jared muttered.

Jared and the old ramrod stood up and walked slowly toward the fire. They were twenty feet away before the young cowboy, Ederly, noticed them.

"We got company, Cole," Ederly said. He took a sip of his coffee.

Cole and Thomas turned to face Jared and Benton. Thomas slowly put down his coffee cup.

"Who the hell are you two?" Cole asked. "Did Snake send ya?"

"No," Jared said coldly.

"Then you'll clear the hell outta here if ya knows what's good fer ya," Cole said.

Thomas looked a bit spooked. He put his hand down by his gun as Jared stepped closer to Cole.

"Do you slap leather as fast as you slap women, asshole?"

"Why, you smart son of a bitch! Yer gonna die!" Cole yelled.

"Draw!" Benton growled.

Edge Cole drew with lightning speed. Jared shifted to the man's left, making him twist and fire off balance. A split second later he had his own gun out. He fanned off two shots so quick it sounded like one.

Cole's bullet tore a hole through Jared's shirt, scoring his left arm. Jared's two shots ripped into Cole's body, one in his shoulder and one in his heart. The Box M man's legs buckled and his head snapped back as he fell into the fire.

Benton took a bullet on the outside of his right thigh but he managed to drill Thomas in the belly, then fanned another shot into his heart.

All through this, young Ederly stood frozen with his coffee cup still in his hand. When it was over, he suddenly realized two guns were aimed at him.

"I didn't shoot at the line shack," he said, his voice cracking with fear. He slowly put his coffee cup down and raised his hands in surrender.

"Is that you, Mr. Jared?" Claire Adams' voice came from across the yard.

"Yes, ma'am," Jared said.

"Can we come out now?"

"Yes, ma'am."

Claire and Celia came out of the shack and over to the fire. They looked down at the two bodies.

"That Mr. Cole was not a very nice man," Claire said.

Jared stared at the bruises on her and Celia's faces.

"Are you alright, Miss Adams?" Benton asked.

"Yes, thank you, Del," she replied. Celia nodded and shivered. She moved closer to her friend.

Young Ederly cleared his throat to speak. "Kin I go?"

"Alright," Benton said. "But if I see ya agin I'll have ta plug ya. Now skedaddle."

Ederly got his horse and mounted up. He sat there staring at the women for a moment.

"Snake Norton an' all the Box M cowboys is headin' this way, Mr. Benton. Better look out fer the ladies."

Ederly nudged his horse into a gallop and was soon lost in the shadows.

"Can you ladies ride?" Jared asked.

"Yes," Celia said. Claire nodded.

"Then we had better move."

"Mr. Jared," Celia said, "Why isn't Mr. Marsh here?"

Jared looked away for a moment then at the old man.

"Miss Celia," Benton said softly, "I had ta give young Bob a Vikin' send off. You know what I'm a-sayin, ma'am?"

"He's dead?"

Benton nodded.

"Oh, dear God!" Celia Grant screamed. "Oh, please no!"

Claire Adams hugged her friend as she shook and cried.

Feeling like intruders, Jared and Benton stepped away for a moment. They reloaded their guns and waited. Celia Grant finally wiped her eyes and cleared her throat.

"I'm ready now," she said.

"If it makes ya feel any better, ma'am, we killed the one what done it."

For Celia Grant there had been too much killing.

Benton led the way. The moon was full and bright above as they came out through the opening in the wall into the field. When they reached the trees on the other side they heard horses behind them, entering the camp from another direction.

"It's Norton," Benton said. "He musta come in from the east through the short cut. We got out jest in time. Let's go!"

They had gone no more than a hundred yards when a band of riders came toward them. It was the Circle C cowboys led by Lee Compton. Benton and Jared rode to meet them.

"Mr. Compton," the old ramrod hollered, "it's all over. We got the girls, sir!"

Claire and Celia came riding up to Compton.

"Are you alright, Claire? Miss Grant?"

"Yes, Lee. We're fine, thanks to Mr. Benton and Mr. Jared."

Benton spoke up. "The Box M raided the east line shack, Mr. Compton. They kilt Bob Marsh and Fuzzy Sanders."

Compton's face was in shadow but his voice told how he felt. "Then we can't let that stand."

"They're setting up an ambush in there," Jared said. "At least wait until daylight."

"No," Compton insisted. "I'm going to get this over with here and now. I'll finish the Box M once and for all. When I'm finished, Madison will never mess with the Circle C again."

"Please, Lee," Celia sobbed. "There's been enough killing. No more, please."

"Let's go home, Lee." Claire began to cry.

Compton reached over and put a hand on Claire's arm. "No need to cry, Claire."

"Don't do this, Lee," Claire pleaded.

"You don't understand, Claire. This is the West. This is how we set things in order, my dear."

"With guns!" Claire blurted out.

"Yes, Claire, with guns."

"But, why?"

"Because the law is far away. Where you live, the law is close by. Day and night, the law is with you. We don't have that luxury here, my dear."

Claire looked at the cowboys gathered behind Lee Compton and shook her head. Compton turned to the old ramrod.

"Take the women home, Del. Keep them safe," Compton said. He smiled at Jared. "Well, Mr. Jared, are you a Circle C cowboy or not? If not, go back with the women and good luck to you, sir."

Jared brought his horse up alongside Compton.

"Are you sure you want to do this?"

"Very sure, Mr. Jared."

"Alright, then, let's get this dance started."

Jared nudged his horse into a walk. Compton and the Circle C cowboys followed. When they came to the entrance, they rode quietly through. Once in, they dismounted and checked their guns. Leaving one man with the horses, they continued on foot. Jared stayed ahead of the others, walking fast. The cowboys had a hard time keeping up with him.

The Box M men were still setting up their ambush when the Circle C cowhands appeared. They were startled by the boldness of their quiet entrance on foot. For a moment they were caught completely off guard.

Jared saw their indecision and made his move.

"Hey!" Jared yelled out, "Where's your ramrod?"

"Here I am, you Circle C asshole!" Snake Norton bellowed like an angry bull as he emerged from the crowd. "Who wants ta know?"

"The Devil does!" Jared said, fanning off three quick shots. He drilled Norton twice in the chest and once between the eyes.

That started the dance.

Guns barked and rifles roared in the moonlit night. Men from both sides dove for cover, running right and left, dodging behind bushes and old mining equipment. Muzzle flashes lit up the area like holiday fireworks. Bullets hit and missed their targets, twanging and ricocheting off into the night. The thud of direct hits were followed by groans of pain as bullets tore through flesh and bone.

"Oh God, oh God!"

"I'm hit, pard!"

"Jesus, I'm blinded!"

"Lord help us all!"

The battle raged on until it hit its apex. Then it slowly ebbed like a wave at low tide going back out to sea. More silence was heard between shots. Men lay scattered on the ground, some dead, some wounded. The wounded groaned in pain. Finally, the last shot was fired and a shroud of silence settled over the mining camp.

Somewhere a pack of coyotes began to wail mournfully as if they knew what man had done to himself.

Signs of dawn began to break in the east. A few buzzards circled high in the morning sky. Soon a dozen or more were wheeling around, staring down at the carnage. Far below, crows squatted in the birches and chatted as if telling their version of the battle.

Clay Jared sat with his back against an old wooden crate. His left arm hung slack. Blood dripped slowly from where a bullet had cut through the upper muscle. He had a second wound in his left thigh that wasn't too bad and a third on the right side of his head. His hat was shot off and he had a groove above his left ear where a bullet plowed through the flesh. The wound stopped bleeding but the side of his face was crusted with blood.

He stared ahead with dull, unseeing eyes.

Suddenly he bent over and threw up. The stench of death was rising quickly in the heat of the sunlight and flies were beginning to gather on the bodies.

A dark shadow walked over to him. He looked up at it.

"You okay, Jared?" It was the old man.

"I'm dead," Jared muttered with his chin on his chest.

"No ya ain't. Ya jest feel like ya are."

"What the hell are you doing here?"

"Ya didn't think I was gonna desert ya, did ya, pard? After all we been through? Hell, we're practically hitched!"

Jared chuckled. He noticed Benton's left arm was bandaged up. He'd been in the fight, too.

Somewhere Jared could hear Claire Adams crying.

"Compton?" he asked.

"Yeah," Benton said. "They shot him all ta ribbons."

The old man helped Jared stand up. The cowboy looked around to locate Claire. He saw her bent over Compton's body. Celia was there too, leaning down, trying to comfort her friend.

"Christ!" was all Jared could say.

He shook his head. "I guess his mom will be real proud of him now," he said sarcastically.

"Yeah," Benton replied in a soft voice. "I'm sure she will."

Jared looked up at the sky. More buzzards were circling above now than before, and others were coming.

18.

The old mining camp became a graveyard. People from both sides came to bury the dead and shake their heads in wonder. All the killing made no sense to them. Local and area newspapers sent reporters and photographers to record the carnage for posterity. The story sold well and was good for their profit line.

Clay Jared was one of only four survivors of that clash of egos and false pride. The land was still there but the angry men were gone.

Both ranches hired new cowboys to fill the empty bunkhouses. Nothing had been gained by the shootout, and the bitterness was still there. Neither side had learned anything, especially not how to get along with each other.

They brought Lee Compton's body back to the Circle C and laid him to rest in the family plot behind the big farmhouse. Ardis Compton asked Claire and Celia to stay on for a while and they agreed to do so.

Celia was still depressed over the loss of young Bob Marsh. One day she cornered the old ramrod.

"Would you please tell me what happened, Mr. Benton?"

The old man nodded. He hesitated a moment, not wanting to be crude or insensitive. Finally, he cleared his throat to speak.

"Well, ma'am, like I said, Bob an' Fuzzy Sanders was ambushed by them Box M skunks, Edge Cole an' his gunnies. Jared and I got there too late ta help, but we managed ta drive 'em off."

The old man sniffed and wiped his nose. His eyes were moist. The recalling of it was painful to him as well.

"Go on," Celia said.

"As Bob lay a-dyin' in my arms he said, 'Don't worry about me, Boss. Go rescue Miss Celia.' Them was his dyin' words, Miss Celia, I swear."

"Then, I was the last person he thought about, before he died?"

"You sure were, ma'am. You were his last thought on this here earth."

The young girl began to sob.

"Did he tell you he wanted a Viking's burial, Mr. Benton?"

"Oh, he sure did, ma'am. An' I did. I gave him the biggest an' best Vikin' send off in the whole world, ma'am. Ya woulda been real proud of it if'n ya was there. Why, them flames reached up an' touched heaven!"

"Really?"

"I swear on my mother's grave, ma'am."

Celia Grant dried her eyes.

"Thank you, Mr. Benton."

She walked slowly up to the house and went in.

The old ramrod stood looking down towards the corral as if he expected to see Bob Marsh sitting on the fence, warming himself in the sun, as he so often liked to do.

But Bob wasn't there anymore.

After her son's death, Ardis Compton's attitude toward Claire and Celia changed. She treated them with more respect. One day, while Celia was listening to Claire playing the piano, Ardis came into the great room.

"Miss Adams, that piece that Lee liked so much? Would you please play it for me?"

"Yes, I would love to," Claire said. "Please call me Claire, Mrs. Compton."

As Claire played Chopin's "Etude in C Minor", Ardis Compton stood at the window and looked out across the yard past the bunkhouse to the fields beyond. She seemed lost in her own thoughts.

When it was over, Mrs. Compton said, "Thank you, Claire," and went up to her bedroom on the second floor. The girls saw that she had been silently crying.

A few days after that, Lee's mother came down from her room dressed to go out.

"I have some business to attend to," she told Claire and Celia. Claire nodded and Mrs. Compton went to the door. She stopped a moment, said something in a low voice without turning around and left.

"What did she just say?" Claire asked Celia.

"I think she said goodbye," Celia replied.

"Are you sure?"

Celia shrugged. Claire went back to playing the piano and Celia picked up a magazine. About a half hour later they heard noises outside. They went to the window and looked out to see Mrs. Compton driving the buckboard out of the yard.

"She must be going to town," Celia said. "She has business there, probably."

But Ardis Compton did not go to town. She headed east. It was a fine spring day. Birds sang in the trees.

Lorne Madison was in his study when he heard a buckboard ride into the yard of the Box M. He stopped working on some papers, got up, and walked to the window to see who it was. His face changed from curiosity to surprise.

"I knew she would come someday," he thought. "It took this to make it happen."

The rancher went to his desk and waited, staring at the door in anticipation. He heard her steps on the porch and then she came in. She closed the door behind her and stood holding her purse in front of her.

"Hello, Lorne," Ardis Compton said.

"Ardis?" It was more a question than a statement, as if he couldn't believe his eyes. He came around the desk and stood facing her. They were but a few feet apart.

"Yes, Lorne, it's me, Ardis."

Madison pointed to a chair.

"Please sit down."

"I'd rather stand, Lorne," Ardis said.

"What brings you here on this fine spring day, Ardis?"

"I'm here to close our book, Lorne."

"What? I don't understand. I don't know what you mean by that."

"Lee is dead. Your men killed him."

"Ardis, your son wasn't supposed to be there. It was just between the men." Madison sighed. "I'm so sorry, Ardis. Believe me. If I was there I would have stopped it. It would never have happened."

"Your son, Lorne...our son."

"What? Our son?"

"Yes. Our son."

The big rancher seemed to shrink in on himself. He looked way for a moment and cleared his throat to speak but didn't. He couldn't think of any words to blunt the blow she had struck him. His massive shoulders sagged.

Finally, he brought himself to look into Ardis Compton's eyes.

"When?"

"That time when Lee's father and the cowboys were out on a trail drive. You didn't go with your men. You stayed behind and waited and then you came and took me. Do you remember that night Lorne?"

The big man nodded yes.

"You threatened to kill Lee's father if I ever told him what you did."

"I loved you. You turned me down for that weakling."

"He was true to me. You weren't half the man he was," Ardis said.

Her words lashed out at him. He groaned in pain and looked away.

"I loved you!" he blurted out.

"No, you took me against my will!"

"Can't you forgive me?"

When he looked back at her, Ardis was pointing a double barreled derringer at his chest.

"For that, yes. But for Lee, no," she said in a calm voice.

She shot Lorne Madison in the heart then shot herself in the left temple.

19.

With his own horse tied to the back of the loaded buckboard and the women up on the bench, Clay Jared snapped the reins and rode out of the yard of the Circle C. The cowboys down by the bunkhouse waved to them. Old Del Norton stood looking as if he was losing his best friend. He knew he'd never see Jared again.

"Good luck, Jared!"

Jared waved but didn't look back. Celia Grant sat very quietly. Claire held her hand but Celia didn't seem to notice. She and Jared made idle talk to pass the time, but the young girl only sat looking straight ahead.

They stopped for the night at Mrs. Simpson's Bed and Breakfast in Fogelsburg. News of the Circle C and Box M range war had already reached town but the old widow didn't know about Bob Marsh's death. When Jared told her, she cried. Celia broke down again. Since learning of the young cowboy's murder, she had never been the same.

They left early in the morning. The sun was shining, the weather was good and the old coach road was smooth.

In a few hours they came to the place where they'd once stopped to eat, where Jared had taught the girls to ride and shoot. Celia started crying again. Claire held her friend in her arms until they were well past the place. It was a long time before the young girl calmed down and dozed off.

They made good time and arrived at the train station in Ellsworth late in the afternoon. Jared pulled the buckboard in close and helped the women get down. He got the bags and put them on the platform near the train.

"I'll go buy the tickets, Mr. Jared," Claire said. Jared nodded and she walked towards the depot office.

Jared noticed two cowboys on the platform several yards away, facing the tracks, waiting for the train to arrive. The tall one stood holding his lariat and the short one had his hand on his gun. His hat sat on the platform a few feet in front of them.

Jared handed Celia Grant a double eagle.

"Go over there and drop it in the hat, Miss Grant."

The young girl looked confused.

"What for?" she asked.

"Go ahead and you'll see."

"Alright."

Jared watched closely as the young girl slowly approached the hat and dropped the coin in. The young cowboy stared at her for a moment, struck speechless by her lovely face.

Finally, he found his voice and said, "Thank you ma'am."

He started to swing his lariat but she stopped him with a soft hand on his.

"Ma'am?" he asked.

"Did you know a cowboy named Bob?"

"Ah, yes ma'am. Thet's my name and thets fer sure."

Celia Grant stared at the cowboy for a moment.

"But you're not Bob Marsh."

"No, ma'am," the cowboy admitted. "My name is Bob Coulter."

"Oh."

"Where are you from, ma'am, if I may ask? From the sound of yer voice I'd say St. Louis."

Celia moved a little closer to the cowboy.

"No, I'm from New York," she said. "But I'm going home now because Bob Marsh died. He was killed in a gunfight protecting me."

"I'm right sorry ta hear thet, ma'am," the cowboy said. "But I sure envy him. It's every cowboy's dream ta die fer a beautiful woman such as yerself."

Claire Adams came back from the depot office with the tickets. They could now hear the train in the distance, heading their way. When she saw Celia she looked alarmed.

"It okay, ma'am," Jared said. "She's in good hands."

The tall cowboy seemed to be telling Celia something. She began to smile and laugh. He twirled his lariat up high into a large loop and dropped it skillfully over them just as the train for Kansas City pulled in and stopped.

People began to debark and others came from the depot to climb aboard.

"Well, Mr. Jared," Claire said. "This has certainly been some experience, I must say."

"We do this all the time," Jared chuckled.

"It's a wonder any of you are alive."

"Yes, it is."

Claire looked across the platform at Celia and yelled to her. The young girl tilted her head up and kissed the startled cowboy on the lips, then ran for the train. The cowboy stood in shock, not believing his luck. His partner howled and slapped him on the back.

Claire turned to Jared.

"I'll miss you, cowboy," she said softly. Her eyes were moist. She kissed Jared softly on the lips and hurried off to get on the train. A porter came from the car and Claire pointed to the bags. He gathered up as much as he could and followed her in, then came back for the rest.

Jared stood on the platform until the train pulled away. He got a last glimpse of the women as their car went out of sight. They waved at him. He sighed, nodded at the two cowboys and walked back to the buckboard.

He found a stable near the train depot and rented a stall for his and the buckboard horse. He spent time with the stable owner and his wife. They had a small kitchen set up behind the stalls and a pot of stew on the stove. He gave them two double eagles and had stew, biscuits and coffee. When it got dark he laid his bedroll out in the back of the buckboard and went to sleep.

In the morning, a rooster crowed and Jared got up. He had a quick breakfast at a nearby beanery and started west for Fogelsburg. Once he got there, he planned to leave the buckboard and horse at Mrs. Simpson's Bed and Breakfast and head for southwest Texas.

With the spring roundup coming, he was sure he could get a job down by Coldwater Creek. If not he'd head further south to Amarillo.

The End

About the Author

As a young boy growing up in the city, R. Annan never passed up a chance to see a western movie. His heroes were Buck Jones, Johnny Mack Brown, Wild Bill Elliot and John Wayne, to name a few. As an adult, he often wondered where his love of westerns came from. Perhaps it has something to do with his grandfather, John L. Annan, who was a cowboy from Helena, Montana, in days of old.

A Note from the Author

Thank you for reading my book. If you enjoyed it, would you please consider rating and reviewing it? I'd enjoy your feedback. Thank you!

Look for other books to appear soon.